ERNIE AND THE FISHFACE GANG

Can Ernie defend the honour of his class and defeat Fishface Duggan and his gang?

Martin Waddell has written many books for children, including the picture books *Farmer Duck* and *Can't You Sleep, Little Bear?*, both of which have won the Smarties Book Prize. Among his many fiction titles are *Cup Final Kid*, *Cup Run*, *Going Up!*, *Shooting Star* and *Star Striker Titch*, and in 2004 he was awarded the prestigious Hans Christian Andersen Award for services to children's literature. Martin lives with his wife Rosaleen in Newcastle, County Down, Northern Ireland.

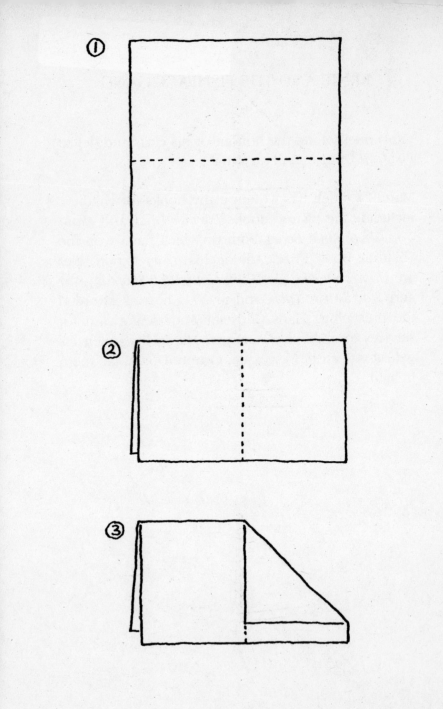

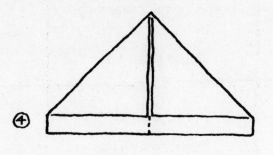

④

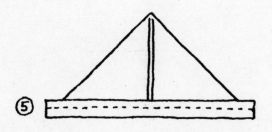

⑤

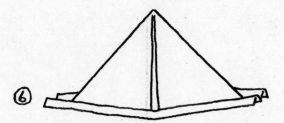

⑥

Books by the same author

Cup Final Kid

Cup Run

Going Up!

Star Striker Titch

MARTIN WADDELL

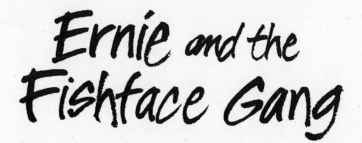

Ernie and the Fishface Gang

Illustrations by Arthur Robins

WALKER
BOOKS

For Dylan

Ernie and the Fishface Gang first published 2002 by Walker Books Ltd
87 Vauxhall Walk, London SE11 5HJ

This edition published 2006

2 4 6 8 10 9 7 5 3 1

Text © 1994 Martin Waddell
Illustrations © 2002 Arthur Robins

The right of Martin Waddell and Arthur Robins to be identified as author
and illustrator respectively of this work has been asserted by them in
accordance with the Copyright, Designs and Patents Act 1988

This book has been typeset in Garamond

Printed and bound in Great Britain by J.H. Haynes & Co. Ltd

British Library Cataloguing in Publication Data:
a catalogue record for this book
is available from the British Library

ISBN-13: 978-1-4063-0622-4
ISBN-10: 1-4063-0622-3

www.walkerbooks.co.uk

CONTENTS

CONTENTS

PEANUT IN THE POND

Peanut Jackson was the smallest P6
in Dingwell Street School.

One morning he was eating crisps
on the way to school when…

Fishface Duggan of P7 got him.
Fishface wasn't alone. He had his
Gang from P7 with him. Rumble and
Mugsy and Ox were the Fishface
Gang, and they all liked crisps. That
was why they ambushed Peanut.

They got the crisps, and they were schoolbag-bashing Peanut, but he did a brilliant bit and got clean away.

He didn't stay clean long.

Right into Dingwell Park duckpond.

The Fishface Gang ran away.

Then along came Ernie Flack and his little brother Dylan on their way to Dingwell Street School through the park.

"Oh look!" said Dylan. "A big duck!"

"That's not a duck," said Ernie, "that's Peanut!"

"Duck!" Dylan said. "Big duck!"

The big duck got up and shook itself, and then it stepped out of the pond. It was a mucky duck, all mud and drips.

"Hello, Duck!" said Ernie.

"Grrrrrrrrrrrr!" said Peanut, shaking himself so that a lot of mud and drips fell on Dylan. Dylan didn't mind. Dylan liked mud.

 "Fishface?" asked Ernie, because it usually was.

"Yes!" said Peanut.

"Revenge!" said Ernie.

"Oh … er," said Peanut.

Ernie Flack was the Hero of P6. He went round righting wrongs like Robin Hood. That is what he told the other P6s anyway, and everyone else at Dingwell Street School, but only Dylan believed him.

They picked up all Peanut's damp things and set off for school.

Outside the park, they met
Ernie's big sister Anna from P7.

"Yeugh!" Anna
said, when
she saw
Peanut.
"Pongy!"
Next they met
Rita and Lorene, the Fighting Lo
Twins.

"Stinky!" said
Rita.

"Smelly!" said
Lorene.

"Who is?"
snapped Peanut.

"You is!" said Rita.

"I can't go in the main gate like this," said Peanut. "Rubberneck will kill me, and then he'll tell my mum." Rubberneck was the deputy head-teacher, Mr Dunlop. He had no hair and some teeth and a lot of temper.

They didn't go in through the gates. They went in through the Ernie Flack School Escape Route instead. It was the hole Ernie had made in the back fence.

When they got inside Ernie hung Peanut out to dry in the bike shed, and went off to deliver Dylan to Reception Class.

"Dylan's dripping," Miss Bluebell said when she saw muddy Dylan.

"Only a bit," said Ernie, and he ran away before Miss Bluebell could tell him to dry Dylan.

"It was the big duck," said Dylan dreamily.

TROUBLE WITH KNEES

Peanut turned up in P6 dressed in an old shirt from the games box and a pair of football shorts that Ernie had stolen from the boys' cloakroom.

"Oh look!" said Mavis. "Sexy knees!"

"You belt up, Mavis Tang!" said Peanut.

"And funny socks!" said Sandra.

"And welly boots!" said Ros.

"I'll thump you!" growled Peanut.

Mavis and Sandra and Ros closed in. They were big, and Peanut was small.

"AHHHHHHHH!" yelled Peanut.
"RESCUE!" yelled Ernie, and he
charged. That is how Ernie Flack
ended up on the floor with Mavis
and Ros and Sandra sitting on him.

Then Mrs Parrot walked in. She was the P6 class teacher. "Bullying the girls, Ernie Flack?" she said, and she picked Ernie up and plonked him in his seat.

"You said nobody would notice my knees!" Peanut said. "*Everybody* did!"

"Oh," said Ernie. He was recovering from being sat on and he wasn't really listening. It is difficult being a hero sometimes.

GROFFEL

At break, Ernie and Peanut had their Get-Even-With-The-Fishfaces Meeting.

"We'll *splat* them!" Ernie said.

"Y-e-s," said Peanut.

"*Destroy* them!" said Ernie, getting more excited.

Peanut didn't say a thing.

"*Revenge!*" cried Ernie. "For the Honour of P6!"

"There are four of them," little Peanut pointed out nervously, "and only two of us. And they are *big!*"

"Rumble isn't very big," said Ernie.

"He's bigger than me!" said Peanut.

"Everybody is bigger than you, Peanut!" Ernie pointed out.

"Mugsy is twice as big as you, and so is Fishface!" said Peanut.

"This needs thinking!" said Ernie.

The Ernie Flack Super Brain went into whirr-power. The result was the P6 Get-Rid-Of-Fishface-For-Ever League, chairperson E. Flack, secretary Peanut.

Ernie told Peanut all about the League while Peanut was getting his clothes off the boiler where Ernie had hung them to dry.

"The Get-Rid-Of-Fishface-For-Ever League!" Ernie announced proudly. "GROFFEL for short. One for all and all for one!"

"So what is the Plan?" Peanut asked, anxiously. The League didn't worry him, because he was used to Ernie's Leagues. It was Ernie's Plans that usually got them into trouble.

"I'm still working on the Plan," Ernie said.

It was dinner time before Ernie had finished working out the Plan. He wrote on Peanut's hand:

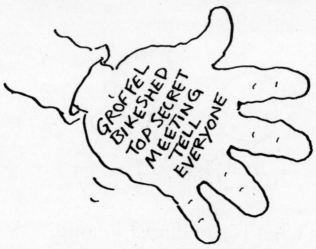

GROFFEL BIKESHED TOP SECRET MEETING TELL EVERYONE

They went around showing it to people.

"What a dirty hand!" said Mavis, but she still came to the shed and so did the Fighting Lo Twins and Rooster and Roker and Beads and Iko and Mo-Mo.

Fishface and his Fishfaces didn't know about the Top Secret Meeting. They had gone down to the goalposts and were playing Meatball with the P3s, which was really nasty because the P3s were the meatballs.

THE PLAN

"This is a Top Secret Meeting to
Save the Honour of P6!" Ernie said,
standing on a bin.

Everybody cheered.

"Peanut must be avenged!" cried Ernie.

This time, not everybody cheered. That was because not everybody liked Peanut. They didn't think they could be bothered avenging him.

"P6 will destroy Fishface Duggan!" Ernie cried.

"Fishface is her boyfriend!" Sandra said, pointing at Mavis.

"Yes, he is!" Mavis said, proudly.

"Mugsy is mine," said Sandra. "And Ros loves Ox, only Ox doesn't know."

"Doesn't matter," said Mavis. "You know what, Ernie Flack? We're going to tell Fishface on you!"

And they ran off to do it.

"Never mind them!" Ernie told the others. "They are traitors to P6. We declare a feud on Fishface and his friends. We must strike *now*, while the iron is hot."

"FREEDOM!" yelled Beads. He was like that.

"Is that the Plan?" Rooster asked.

"Yes," said Ernie. "Good, isn't it?"

There was a long silence.

"Kind of good anyway," said Ernie. "It will be good when we…"

But everybody else had gone, except Peanut.

"Looks like 'we' means 'us'," said Peanut. "You and me!"

"You and me and Dylan," said Ernie.

"I don't think Dylan counts," said Peanut.

ON THE RUN

"Fishface knows!" Sandra hissed to Ernie, just before the end-of-school bell.

Fishface did.

Fishface was after them.

Ernie and Peanut only just escaped from the cloakroom on time. Then they had to use Miss Bluebell for cover when they were fetching Dylan from Reception.

They made it out of school by
the School Escape Route. Then
they had to go right the way up
Dingwell Street.

They crept along, ducking into
doorways and keeping a special
Fishface lookout all the way.

"Where are they?" hissed Ernie.

"Somewhere," said Peanut, nervously. "Somewhere, waiting to grab us."

"Who is?" asked Dylan. He was still wearing the paper hat which Miss Bluebell had helped him to make in Reception. He felt happy because he had a hat to show Mum.

"Do we *have* to go through the park?" Peanut whispered.

Dylan stopped.

Dylan liked the park. His friends from Reception played in the park on their way home, and he wanted to play with them.

"Well…" said Ernie.

Dylan opened his mouth to scream. He had his Dylan-scream face on, but Ernie saw it just in time.

"We have to go through the park,"
Ernie said.

Dylan smiled.

Dylan skipped ahead through the
park gates, swinging his tiny
schoolbag.

Peanut grabbed him and shoved
him into the bushes.

"They'll spot us!" Peanut gasped.

Then Ernie's Super Brain whirred.

Somewhere, out in the park, the Fishface Gang waited.

Sooner or later the Fishface Gang would grab them.

But … Ernie's Super Brain had the answer.

"Dylan wants to play," Ernie said.

"But they'll spot him!" gasped Peanut.

"Off you go, Dylan," said Ernie.

Dylan burst out of
the bushes, waving
his schoolbag and
holding tightly
onto his paper hat
to stop it blowing
away.

Dylan headed up the path
towards the sandpit, and straight
into it.

The path led round the sandpit,
and to the "Way Out" gate they
were heading for. It was getting
past the sandpit and down the rest
of the path to the gate that
presented problems.

THE FISHFACE GANG'S LAST STAND

The big bush beside the path shook.

It wasn't the wind. It was the Fishfaces, waiting to grab Ernie and Peanut.

"What do we do now?" Peanut gasped.

"I want to play with Dylan!" Ernie said.

And the next moment he emerged from the bushes, strolling straight up the middle of the path towards the sandpit where Dylan and the tinies were digging castles and playing about with all the mums and dads and ladies-who-come-to-collect-you-from-school.

"They're going to grab us, Ernie!" Peanut whispered.

"Just keep moving," said Ernie. "When they try to grab us, do what I do!"

He didn't get to say any more, because at that moment Fishface Duggan yelled, "Charge!" and Fishface and Mugsy and Ox and Rumble came yelling and screaming out of the bushes waving their schoolbags.

"Run!" Ernie yelled. He headed straight for the sandpit full of tinies!

Ernie and Peanut were ahead of the Fishface Gang, but the Gang were gaining fast. Then Ernie swerved at the last minute and ran round the sandpit.

"Cut them off!" yelled Fishface.
"Get them at the other side!"

The Fishfaces didn't mess about.
They didn't run round the sandpit
after Ernie and Peanut. They
headed straight across it, to cut off
Ernie's escape route to the gate.

Fishface didn't even notice the tinies. Fishface never did. They charged straight across without a thought for anything else.

Tinies screamed! Tinies screeched! Tinies started lashing out with their buckets and spades and getting tangled up in running feet. Tinies yelled! Tinies wailed!

Suddenly the sandpit wasn't full of the Fishface Gang jumping over tinies and their castles in pursuit of Peanut and Ernie. It was full of mums and dads and ladies-who-

come-to-collect-you-from-school
waving big handbags and
umbrellas and bags of shopping
and briefcases, charging after the
Fishface Gang.

Mums and dads and ladies-who-
come-to-collect-you-from-school
and tinies and Fishfaces were
rolling around in the sand.

The mums and dads and ladies-who-come-to-collect-you-from-school were on top, and the Fishfaces were underneath.

Then Rubberneck came dashing
into the park, followed by Mrs
Parrot, and the four angry mums
who had fetched them from
school. It was the Fishface Gang's
Last Stand.

The mums and dads and ladies-
who-come-to-collect-you-from-
school and tinies with their buckets
and spades all marched out of the
park, led by Rubberneck and Mrs
Parrot, taking the Fishface Gang to
their doom.

That left Peanut and Ernie and
Dylan.

Dylan was covered in sand and
glory because he had been right in
the middle of the sandpit battle,
but Ernie and Peanut weren't.

They had been sitting on the grass by the park gate, watching.

"We won!" said Ernie.

"It was the mums and dads and ladies," said Peanut. "Not us!"

"Who led the Fishfaces into the sandpit trap?" said Ernie.

"We did!" said Peanut.

"One for all, and all for mums!"
said Ernie, and they went home
with Dylan trotting behind them
swinging his schoolbag and trying
to look innocent.

Dylan had been busy after the battle in the sandpit. His schoolbag was full of other tinies' paper hats.

The hats were a present for his mum.

Dylan had fourteen paper hats.
He didn't know he had fourteen
paper hats because he could only
count to five, but he knew he had
a lot of hats and that made him
happy.

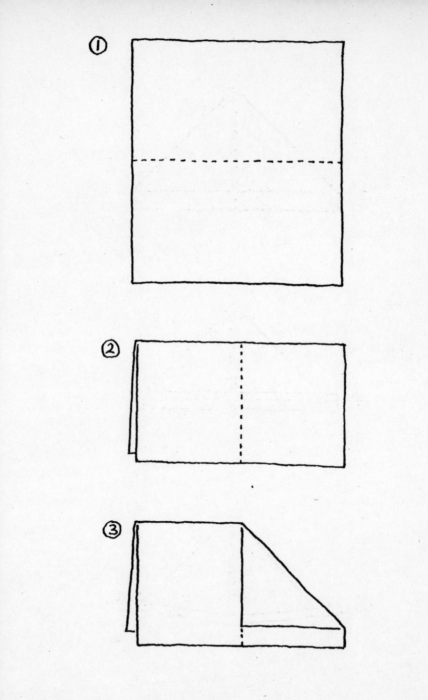

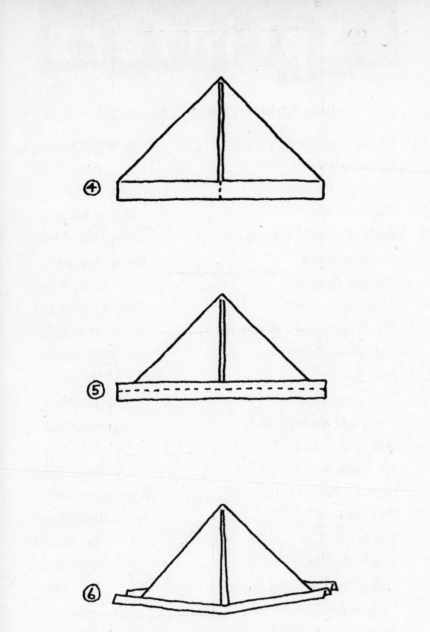

④

⑤

⑥

Fun Sprinters for you to enjoy!